Sumac and the Magic Lake

CHARACTERS

Narrator 1	Farmer's Son 2
Narrator 2	Sumac
Emperor	Sparrow 1
Empress	Sparrow 2
Farmer	
Farmer's Wife	
Farmer's Son 1	

SETTING

An ancient Inca empire

Narrator 1: The Inca once ruled a powerful kingdom. This tale is about an Inca emperor whose only son was very ill.

Narrator 2: The best doctors in the land were called to help him. But none could find a cure.

Emperor: Our only child! What are we to do? What if he dies? Who will rule the land when we are gone?

Empress: Do not fear. We will find a way to save him.

Emperor: This morning I heard a voice coming from the fire. But I must have been dreaming.

Empress: Or perhaps the gods want to help us. What did the fire say to you?

Emperor: The fire spoke of a magic lake at the end of the Earth. It said that if our son drinks from its waters, he will be cured.

Empress: We must find that lake!

Emperor: But how? Even if there is such a lake, we cannot leave our son to look for it.

Empress: Do not give up hope. We will find a way.

Narrator 1: The emperor spread the word all over the land. Anyone who found the magic lake at the end of the Earth would get a reward.

Narrator 2: Whoever found the lake would save the prince.

Narrator 1: At the same time, a farmer shared his own worries with his family.

Farmer: Another year with so little rain! Our crops will be ruined.

Farmer's Wife: Do not worry! We will get by.

Farmer's Son 1: Father, we have news! The emperor will reward anyone in the kingdom who finds a magic lake to cure the prince.

Farmer's Son 2: We are going to look. We will find the magic lake.

Farmer's Son 1: And our worries will be over!

Farmer: But it is almost harvest time. I will need your help in the field. Even our small farm is too big for your mother, your sister Sumac, and I to work alone.

Sumac: Father, I am strong. I can work in the field. Let them go.

Farmer's Son 2: Please, Father. We will be back in time to help you.

Farmer's Son 1: Yes, Father. We promise. If we do not find the magic lake in a month, we will come home.

Farmer's Wife: Let them try. They just want to help the prince and our family.

Farmer: All right. But do not forget. The harvest begins in one month. Be back by then.

Farmer's Wife: I just want you back safe and sound.

Narrator 2: So the brothers set off. They walked many miles each day.

Farmer's Son 2: It has been almost one month, Brother. And no magic lake! We must start back soon.

Farmer's Son 1: Look at that sparkling pool of water over there. I say we bring back some of its water for the Emperor's son.

Farmer's Son 2: Why? That is not the magic lake.

Farmer's Son 1: I know. But the water is so clean and lovely. If the prince thinks it is magic, it may help him.

Farmer's Son 2: It can't hurt to try. All right. Let us take some water.

Narrator 2: They filled their jugs with the lake water.

Narrator 1: Then they went to the palace.

Empress: You say you found the magic lake, and this is its water?

Farmer's Son 1: Yes, Empress.

Emperor: It doesn't look special.

Empress: And it is not working. Our son is still ill.

Emperor: These brothers are trying to trick us. Guards! Throw them in jail!

Farmer's Son 2: No, no! What will our family do now?

Narrator 2: The farmer and his wife heard the bad news.

Farmer's Wife: Oh, no! Our sons tried to trick the emperor!

Farmer: What will become of them? What will we do about the harvest?

Sumac: I will go find the magic lake, Father. Please let me try. The water may save the prince. It may save my brothers' lives now, too!

Farmer's Wife: We must let her try. What choice do we have?

Narrator 1: That day, Sumac set off in search of the magic lake.

Narrator 2: That night, she went to sleep in a tall tree.

Sumac: The wild animals will leave me alone up here. Maybe tomorrow I will find the magic lake.

Sparrow 1: The girl is brave to be out here alone.

Sumac: Hello, beautiful sparrows! Would you like to share some of my corn?

Sparrow 2: What a sweet girl! We must try to help her.

Sparrow 1: Yes. But what can we do?

Sparrow 2: We'll each give her a feather from our wings. She can make a magic fan with them.

Sparrow 1: That is a wonderful idea!

Sparrow 2: Please, take these feathers. Spread the feathers out like a fan. They will carry you to the magic lake and protect you.

Sumac: Thank you, sparrows! Here I go!

Narrator 2: In no time, Sumac arrived at the magic lake. But her troubles were not over.

Sumac: Oh! What are those awful monsters coming toward me? Help me, Magic Fan!

Narrator 1: Sumac waved the fan at the giant lake monsters. Soon, they were asleep by the shore.

Sumac: That was close. I must leave before they wake up.

Narrator 1: Sumac filled a vessel with the magic lake water. Then she said ...

Sumac: To the palace, please, Magic Fan!

Narrator 2: In the blink of an eye, she was at the sick prince's side.

Narrator 1: Sumac helped the prince sip the magic water. He was well again!

Empress: You saved our son!

Emperor: Thank you, child! Whatever riches you wish for are yours.

Sumac: I would like three favors instead, please.

Empress: Name them.

Sumac: First, will you forgive my brothers and free them? They meant no harm. They were just trying to help our family.

Emperor: Certainly. It is done.

Sumac: Also, I would like to return the magic feathers to the sparrows.

Sparrow 1: We are right here to claim them, Sumac.

Sparrow 2: We have been with you all along.

Sparrow 1: But now we must get back to the forest. Never forget the magic that your kindness brought you.

Empress: Please name your third wish, Sumac.

Sumac: My parents have a farm in the mountains. I love it there. But without rain, we have no food to sell or to eat.

Emperor: Say no more. I know just what to do.

Narrator 2: It was now time for Sumac to go home.

Narrator 1: Her parents and brothers were waiting for her at home.

Narrator 2: So were a dozen llamas!

Farmer: Look, Sumac! The llamas will help us plow the fields and get the crops planted on time. Even if the rain does not come, we will be able to sell llama wool!

Narrator 2: Sumac and her family lived happily ever after.

Narrator 1: Since those days long ago, no one has seen the magic lake again.

The End